NOW SHEBA SINGS THE SONG

by MAYA ANGELOU

with art by TOM FEELI

E. P. Dutton | Dial Books

New York

Published by E.P. Dutton | Dial Books
2 Park Avenue | New York, New York 10016
Published simultaneously in Canada by Fitzhenry & Whiteside Limited, Toronto

Text copyright © 1987 by Maya Angelou
Art copyright © 1987 by Tom Feelings
All rights reserved | Printed in the U.S.A.
Typography by Jane Byers Bierhorst
First Edition
W
3 5 7 9 10 8 6 4 2

Library of Congress Cataloging-in-Publication Data

Angelou, Maya | Now Sheba sings the song

I. Feelings, Tom. II. Title.
PS3551.N464N67   1987   811'.54   86-19876
ISBN 0-525-24501-4

*To all my black, brown,
beige, yellow, red, and white sisters*

M.A.

*To all the women in my family,
especially my mother Anna, my sister Flo,
my aunts Julia and Dolly, and to the
memory of my buddy Julian Mayfield,
a man who truly loved women*

T.F.

Introduction

These drawings of Black women were made over the course of twenty-five years. They were all drawn from life, on the spot, in many places in Africa, America, South America, and the Caribbean Islands.

These are ordinary women, what I call extraordinary ordinary women. They are not models—not in the western sense, but to me they are far more beautiful.

They are all different, separate and individual, real women. Some, especially those born in South and North America, are of mixed blood: Native American, East Indian, Oriental, Amerindian, Spanish, Portuguese, and other Europeans. But these women too—all of the women—have Africa's blood flowing through them.

In my artwork I wanted to show the fluid energy, the rhythmic movements of the women, and in almost all of them the strong presence of a definite dance consciousness in their lives. So the original art was all done in flowing black line, and the line, I hope, reflects this rhythm.

I worked sepia tones into the drawings and tried to bring them all together as a group, to connect the line with tone and with volume above and below the surface of the paper—to connect these women from afar. The sepia, the dark brown, the light brown, shows that no matter what color they really are or what particular features they possess, no matter what the form, the content, the spirit, the woman inside these women reflects the continent of Africa.

Some were born and raised far from Africa, in different parts of the world, but they all vividly remind me of Africa's past and present history—beautiful, but reflecting painful experiences, sometimes dehumanizing experiences. Even if they chose not to show it, you would think this pain would inform their faces in a negative way. Yet there is a strength and more, an openness in these women's gaze, in the way they look and hold themselves that produces a wonderful sense of balance. I am still awed by it.

Right from the beginning, these drawings were done at random—wherever I went, in cafes, nightclubs, shops, marketplaces, homes, on the streets, in schools, day-care centers, hospitals, and all types of public transportation—everywhere. I tried to capture a sense of the primal importance of Black women, fueled by my growing awareness of their strength and beauty, so undervalued in the world.

Over the years I held on to all this artwork...feeling that each piece had within it a connecting thread, a link that could tie them all together into a collective storyline. But who could tell this story? It had to be someone who was aware of Africa's complex and diversified importance to world history and the role of Africa's women as its rich source of nurturing power. It had to be someone who loved that source as her own. I thought back to the early 1960s when I left America's racial problems and departed for Africa, and my own early days of living in Ghana, West Africa, where I felt for the first time in my life a part of a majority. I thought back to how I immersed myself in Africa's natural blackness, gaining strength in my convictions through working for the government as an illustrator and daily soaking in all the things my eyes yearned to see. One lazy warm afternoon as I stood on the side of a road waiting for a bus, the sun in my face, feeling warm and alive, I looked at a middle-aged Ghanaian woman standing next to me with all her kitchenwares piled amazingly and gracefully high on her head. She flashed a sunlit smile at me, one that can only come out of Africa, and I saw that she was blue-black in color. Her skin was wet and sparkling with perspiration, actively reflecting the light of day, and she was shining all over and glowing with a rich dark purple hue that pushed its way up gently from deep within her. I knew at that moment that all I had heard, read, and been taught in America about Black being ugly—was a lie. For based on those values this woman was supposed to be ugly...yet I was looking at the most beautiful sight my eyes had ever seen.

For me at that moment all of Africa's beauty and majesty was there in this woman...and as an artist and as a *man* that's what I had come to Africa to see, feel, and have affirmed.

But now in the mid-1980s I thought about who could tell this *woman's* story and all the other stories locked inside the faces of all the women in my drawings...from their perspective. It had to be someone who shared a similar experience, someone who traveled, opened up, took in, and mentally recorded everything observed. And most important of all, it had to be someone whose *center* is woman. My mind went immediately to a good friend I had met in Ghana twenty years earlier—Maya Angelou.

I took the artwork to her. The enthusiasm she showed on seeing the drawings let me know right away that I had come to the right place. I gave her the drawings to study, without asking or suggesting what she thought she might do. For half a year the drawings were in Maya's study, on the floor, on the walls, on chairs, and every ready surface. She was living with them now and finally one day...the wonderful poem was finished, and Maya Angelou had given these women their sound, their voices—to match their beauty.

For a long time I thought that because I had lived and traveled in Africa I was able to see clearly the great quality of power, openness, and balance that so struck me in Black women...but when I came back to America and looked into the face of my mother I saw it all there. Then I was reminded that it had always been there, in her eyes and in my grandmother's eyes too.

It had only been clouded by *my* experience of living in America. Finally I understood that Africa's beauty, strength, and dignity is wherever the Black woman is. For Africa, Mother Africa, gave birth to us all.

Tom Feelings

NOW SHEBA SINGS THE SONG

Mother told her secrets to me
When I rode
Low in the pocket
Between her hips.

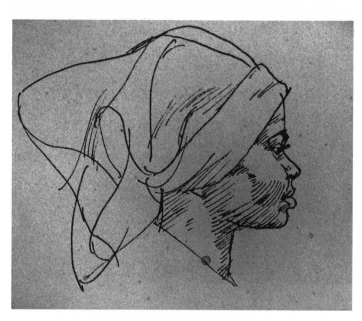

I learned the rhythm of her song
"Child, this world is not your home."
History does not dissolve
In the blood.

All my ways of being are musical and mysterious.
Yet I embrace you openly.
Ripe with expectancy.

My eyes, reflecting the Limpid Limpopo
Look beyond the past
For my children whose future rest on their closed eyelids.

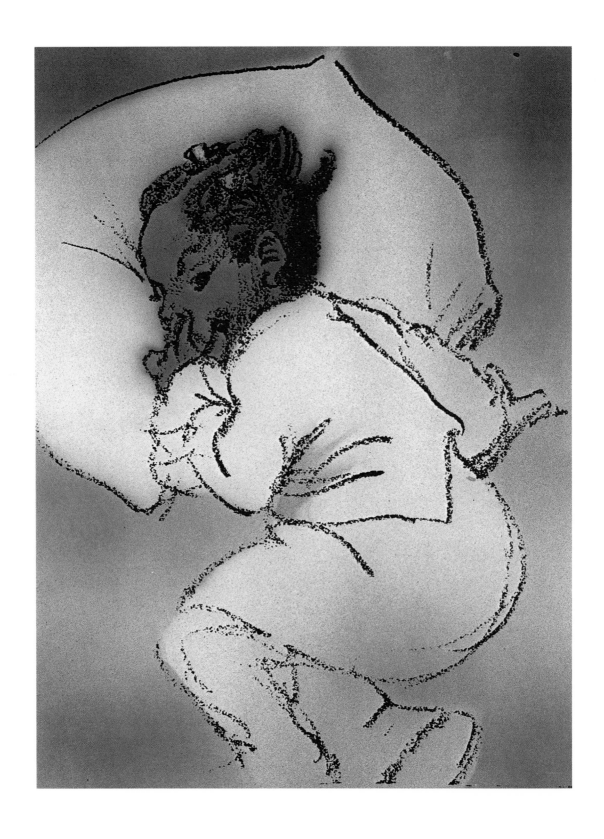

Centuries have recorded my features, in Cafes and
    Cathedrals, along the water's edge.
I awaited the arrival the ships of freedom
On the selling stage as men proved their power in a
    handful of my thigh.

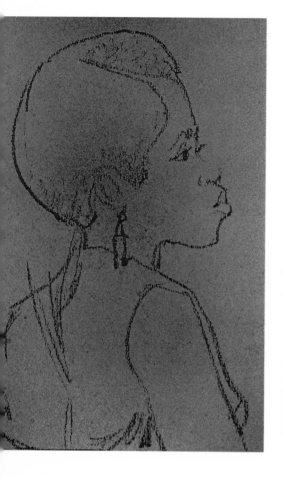  

Across my peach flesh lips I blow river boats on the skin
    of the Mississippi.
And feluccas up the ancient Nile.
Clouds race from my peanut butter colored puffed cheeks.

My breasts
Are the fulness of mangos
In a royal forest
Constant, swaying, jungle flowers.

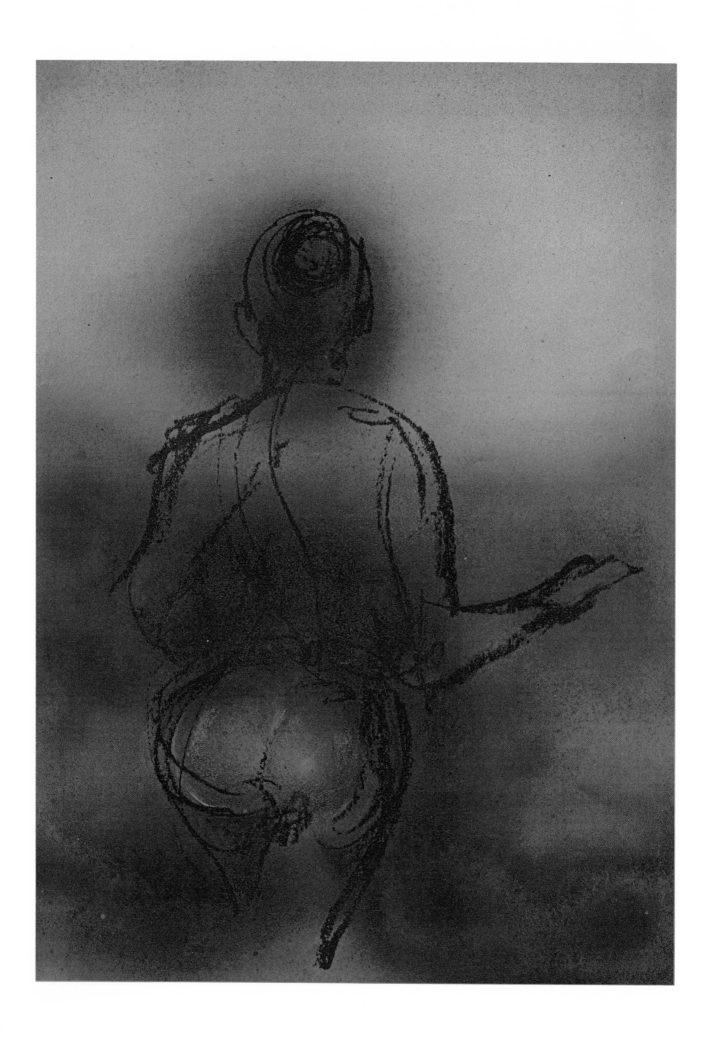

My impertinent buttocks
(High, redolent, tight as dark drums)
Send the wind to shake tall grasses
Introduce frenzy into the hearts of small men.

From the columns of my thighs
I take the strength to hold the world aloft
Standing, too often, with a cloud of loneliness
Forming halos for my head.

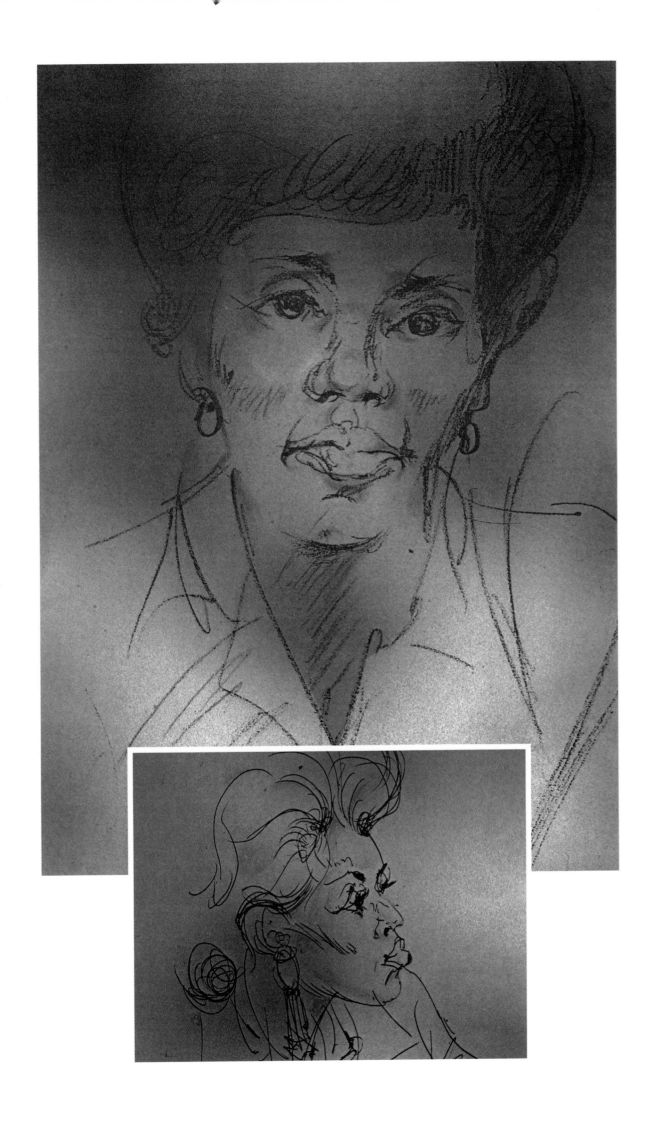

Oaks, massive with the memory of Lynch
Perversions, bend to grip my knees and rustle
A moan for our burned visions.
The trees may weep. I must stiffen my back
Quieten my face and teach a lesson in Grace.

I do get tired and wonder
When my change is going to come.
But if the Lord says so
And the creek don't rise I know
I'll get better, better.

What I have not seen cannot be.
Sunsets and rainbows, green forest and restive blue seas, all
    naturally colored things are my siblings. We have played
    together on the floor of the world
Since the first stone looked up
At the stars.

Innocence, as riches, plates my
Skin all carats gold, beckons
Lust and leers and on the delicious occasion my lover
   whose talent convinces me away from fear.

My hair, a hive of honey bees
Is a queenly glory
Crackles like castanets
Hums like marimbas.

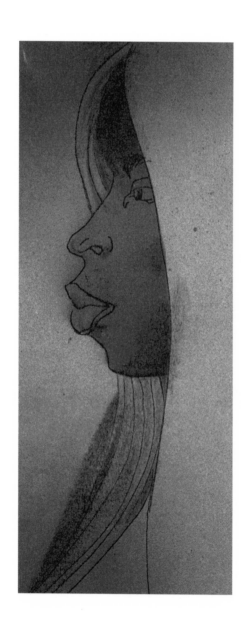

Oh my movement admits to
Lip smacking, finger snapping, toe tapping
Shoulder bouncing, hip throwing, breast thrusting, eye
    flashing,
Love of good and God and Life.

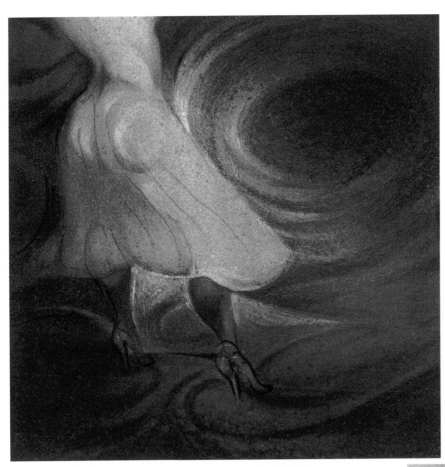

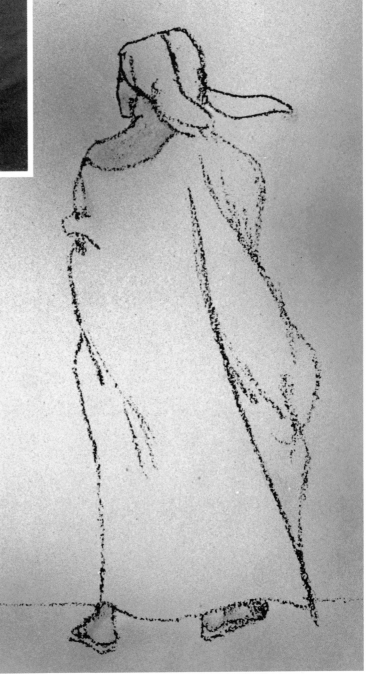

My songs wreathe the people in banners
Of hope, of wisdom and some just plain laughing out loud

I know the near and distant peaks
Ridges and crevices, aretes and tors
Valleys, chasms, gulleys of which I am made
Are strewn with remorse, pain, triumph and ecstasy.

I am mate to Kilimanjaro
Fujiyama, Mont Blanc and Sister to Everest
He who is daring and brave will know what to do.

DATE DUE

	PRINTED IN U.S.A.